"What you learn at an HBCU is you do not have to fit into somebody's limited perspective on what it means to be young, gifted, and black."

-VPOTUS Kamala Harris

I SEE YOU HBCU

Written by Keyshawn McMiller
Illustrated by Bryan McMillan

"Ahman, pick up that tablet."

"Ahman, don't forget your lucky shoes."

"No, Ahman, we can't take the house with us."

Ahman and his parents were moving into a larger home. Tired of lifting boxes all Ahman wanted to do was explore.

Zigzagging in and out of rooms, he looked at the writing on the boxes, "Kitchen," "Entertainment," "Bathroom." He stopped when he saw a box with a strange word on it, "HBCU."

HBCU

Alone, Ahman excitedly opened the box and touched the colorful clothed trinkets, and pictures of Black faces. He put on a hat that read "HBCU" in large maroon letters and ran his parents.

"What's this, what's this!?" Ahman shouted.

"Ahman, we've got to pack, not un-pack." His dad groaned.

"C'mon, let's take a break, Sirus." His mom said as she walked Ahman to the couch.

"Anything for you, momma." his dad sighed.

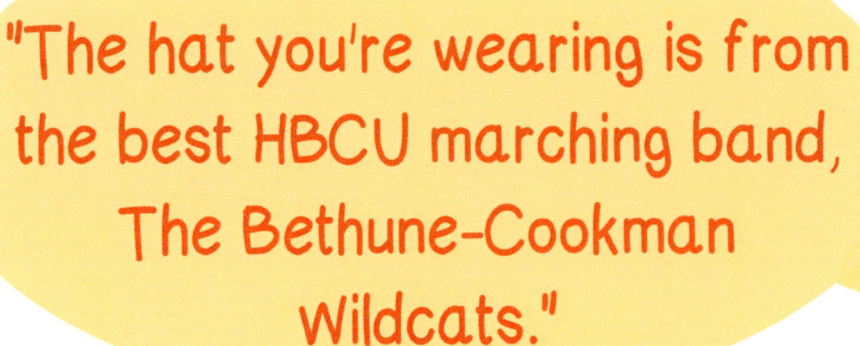

"The hat you're wearing is from the best HBCU marching band, The Bethune-Cookman Wildcats."

Ahman's dad suddenly marched around the living room, humming tunes of the past.

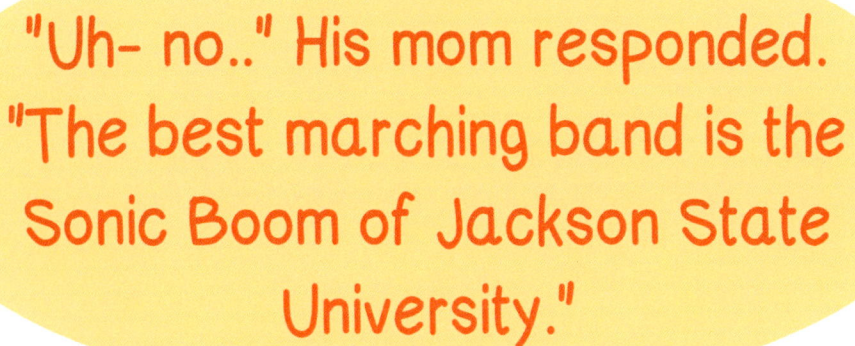

"Uh- no.." His mom responded. "The best marching band is the Sonic Boom of Jackson State University."

His mom did a dance, and Ahman smiled.

"Wow! What's an HPCU?" he asked.

"H-B-C-U stands for Historically Black College and University." His mom replied.

Ahman learned that there was a time where Black students could not go to school with White students.

HBCUs gave Black students a chance to learn.

"Yes." Ahman's dad said.

"There are over 100 HBCUs in the United States. Each school has its own special swag and history. But they all improve the lives of all of Black and Brown students."

"I want to know them all!" he shouted.

Ahman's parents looked at each other and smiled.

"Alright, little man, hand me my laptop." His father said.

Ahman sat with his parents hearing about each of the 101 HBCU's.

He learned of Mary McLeod Bethune's $1.50 and 7 girls and Jackson State University's motto of Challenging Minds and Changing Lives.

He was amazed learning Edward Waters College was the first HBCU in Florida.

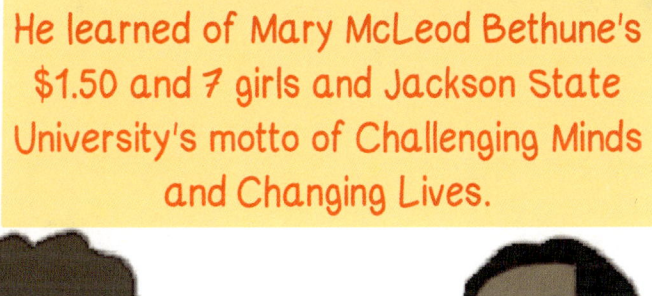

Fisk University has a world-famous choir.

Howard University was where Vice President of the United States, Kamala Harris, went to.

"I want to go to an HBCU!" Ahman cried. to."

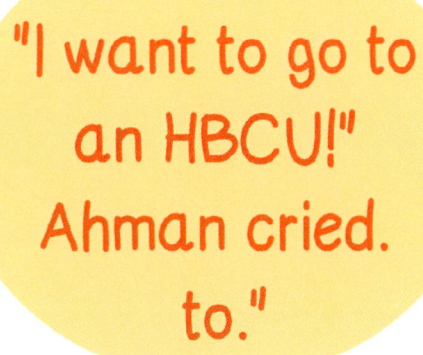

His parents hugged him and said, "You can do anything you set your mind to."

That night, Ahman dreamed of his own HBCU adventure. He wanted a chance at achieving Black Excellence and to share it with his kids too.

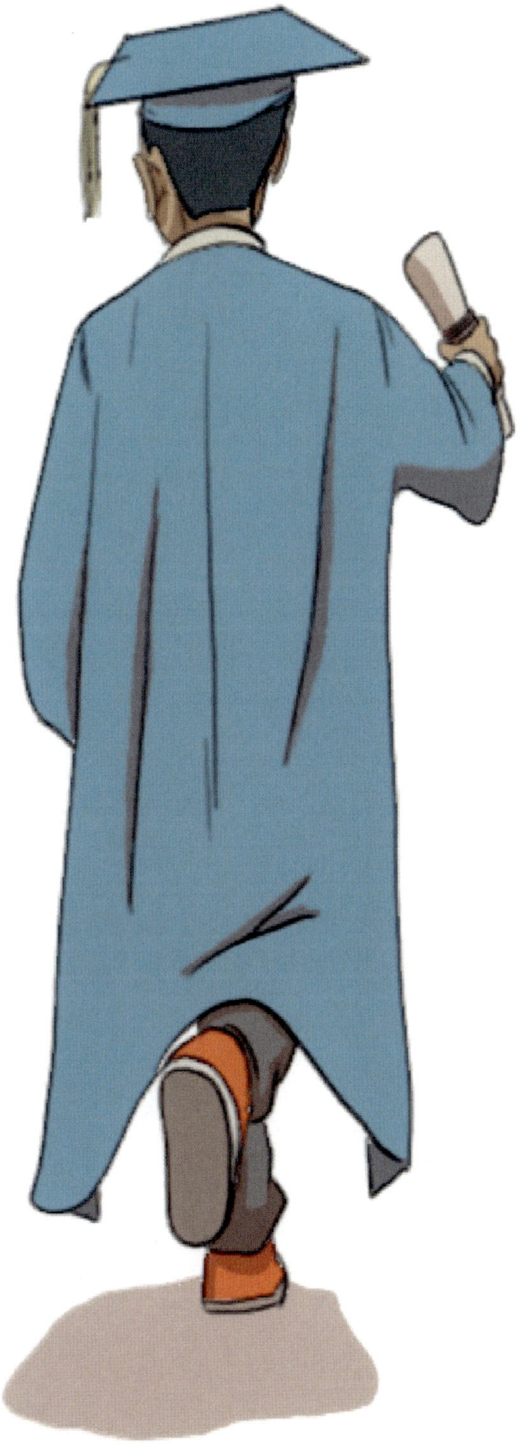

This book is dedicated to the 107 HBCUS, past and present. They span 22 states from California to the Virgin Islands. They have produced pioneers and industry shapers in medicine, law, education, music, journalism, theater, science, art, technology, engineering, social science, mathematics, and every other area in between. To those who are fortunate enough to have an HBCU adventure of their own, cherish it with all your might. Share it with the next generation. Share it with the world, for there is truly nothing quite like it...

Complete list of 107 HBCUS
(thehundred-seven.org, 2022)

Alabama

Alabama A&M University- Huntsville
Alabama State University- Montgomery
Concordia University-Alabama- Selma
Gadsden State College- Gadsden
J.F. Drake State Technical College- Huntsville
Lawson State Community College- Birmingham
Miles College- Fairfield
Miles School of Law- Fairfield
Oakwood University- Huntsville
Selma University- Selma
Shelton State Community College- Tuscaloosa
Stillman College- Tuscaloosa
Talladega College- Talladega
Tuskegee University- Tuskegee
H. Councill Trenholm State Community College- Montgomery

Arkansas
University of Arkansas at Pine Bluff- Pine Bluff
Arkansas Baptist College- Little Rock
Philander Smith College- Little Rock
Shorter College- North Little Rock

Delaware
Delaware State University- Dover

District of Columbia
University of the District of Columbia
Howard University

Florida
Bethune Cookman University- Daytona Beach
Edward Waters University- Jacksonville
Florida A&M University- Tallahassee
Florida Memorial University- Miami Gardens

Georgia
Albany State University- Albany
Carver College*- Atlanta
Clark Atlanta University- Atlanta
Fort Valley State University- Fort Valley
Interdenominational Theological Center- Atlanta
Johnson C Smith Theological Seminary- Atlanta
Morehouse College- Atlanta
Morehouse School of Medicine- Atlanta
Morris Brown College- Atlanta
Paine College- Augusta
Savannah State University- Savannah
Spelman College- Atlanta

Kentucky
Kentucky State University- Frankfort
Simmons College of Kentucky- Louisville

Louisiana
Dillard University-New Orleans
Grambling State University- Grambling
Southern University and A&M College- Baton Rouge
Southern University New Orleans- New Orleans
Southern University-Shreveport- Shreveport
Xavier University- New Orleans

Maryland
Bowie State University- Bowie
Coppin State University- Baltimore
University of Maryland- Eastern Shore- Princess Anne
Morgan State University- Baltimore

Michigan
Lewis College of Business- Detroit

Mississippi
Alcorn State University- Lorman
Coahoma Community College- Clarksdale
Hinds County Community College- Utica
Jackson State University- Jackson
Mississippi Valley State University- Itta Bena
Rust College- Holly Springs
Tougaloo College- Tougaloo

Missouri
Harris-Stowe State University- St. Louis
Lincoln University- Jefferson City

North Carolina
Barber-Scotia College- Concord
Bennett College- Greensboro
Elizabeth City State University- Elizabeth City
Fayetteville State University- Fayetteville
Hood Theological Seminary- Salisbury
Johnson C. Smith University- Charlotte

Livingstone College- Salisbury
North Carolina Central University- Durham North Carolina
A&T State University- Greensboro
Shaw University- Raleigh
St. Augustine's University- Raleigh
Winston-Salem State University- Winston Salem

Ohio
Central State University- Wilberforce
Payne Theological Seminary- Wilberforce
Wilberforce University- Wilberforce

Oklahoma
Langston University- Langston

Pennsylvania
Cheyney University- Cheyney
The Lincoln University- Lincoln University

South Carolina
Allen University- Columbia
Benedict College- Columbia
Claflin University- Orangeburg
Clinton College- Rock Hill
Denmark Technical College- Denmark
Morris College- Sumter
South Carolina State University- Orangeburg
Voorhees University- Denmark

Tennessee
American Baptist University- Nashville
Fisk University- Nashville
Knoxville College- Knoxville
Lane College- Jackson

LeMoyne Owen College- Memphis
Meharry Medical College
Tennessee State University- Nashville

Texas
Huston-Tillotson University- Austin
Jarvis Christian College- Hawkins
Paul Quinn College- Dallas
Prairie View A&M University- Prairie View
Southwestern Christian College- Terrell
St. Philip's College- San Antonio
Texas College- Tyler
Texas Southern University- Houston
Wiley College- Marshall

US Virgin Islands
University of the Virgin Islands- St. Thomas & St. Croix

Virginia
Hampton University- Hampton
Norfolk State University- Norfolk
Saint Paul's College- Lawrenceville
Virginia State University- Petersburg
Virginia Union University- Richmond
Virginia University of Lynchburg- Lynchburg

West Virginia
Bluefield State College- Bluefield
West Virginia State University- Institute

About the Writer

Keyshawn McMiller earned a Bachelors of Social Work degree from The Florida A&M University and marched for The Bethune-Cookman Wildcats of Bethune-Cookman University. Empowered by his motto of "moving, growing, learning, and enjoying life," Keyshawn walks alongside others towards manifesting their best selves through counseling, research, and community-based programming.

Other Works by Keyshawn McMiller

- Ideals From A Young Black Introvert: A Mini-Guide To A Better Life
- Winnas: A Black Males' Path to a King's Mentality

Made in the USA
Middletown, DE
17 October 2022